T0198882

Flash's Choice

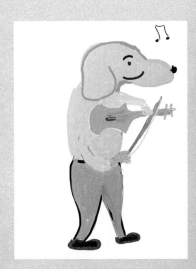

Charlie Alexander

Flash's Choice

Written by Charlie Alexander

Flash's Choice

Written by Charlie Alexander
Art work by Charlie Alexander

Driving the school bus
was a big responsibility.

Flash knew how important it is to
be safe.

There was a long line.

Lots of hopes for a good job!

Flash wore his best suit!

This interview was very important!

Fighting fires!

Flash volunteered to help!

Flash stood at attention!

You're in the army now!

The barbell was so heavy.

Flash lifted it anyway!

Playing the Violin was fun.

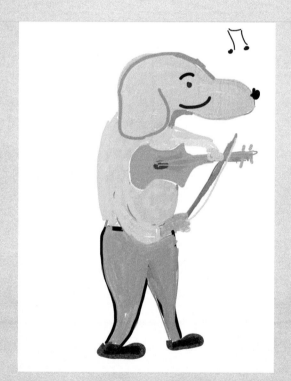

It helped Flash relax and smile!

Flash was a fine carpenter.

He really nailed it this time!

Flash tried to play baseball!

Walking for a run was so confusing!

He was flying through the clouds.

Flash was a very good pilot!

Dog walking was a cool job.

Flash made sure the leash was secure!

Flash shot an arrow!

Luckily it was on target.

Flash tried to dunk it!

Score two points for Flash!

Please obey the law!

Flash was a very fair judge!

Flash gave the baby a bath.

He had to dry the baby and himself!

Mowing the lawn is needed.

Flash has already mowed three yards!

Flash tossed the horseshoe.

He was a real ringer!

Fixing telephone wires was a dangerous job.

Flash was very careful climbing the ladder.

There was lots of mail.

Flash carefully placed the envelopes in each mailbox.

The race track was crowded!

Flash had to keep both hands on the wheel.

Flash went scuba diving.

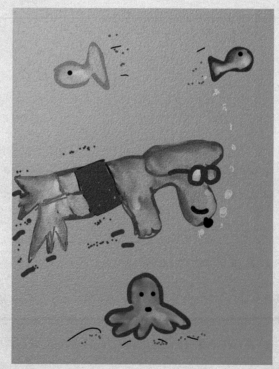

He liked his goggles and fins!

A strike or a spare will win.

Flash rolled the ball right down the middle.

Flash got a new racquet!

He easily hit the tennis ball over the net.

Flash was cutting down a tree.

It wasn't easy to be a lumberjack!

Flash liked watching Birds.

He enjoyed looking through his binoculars.

Making coffee smelled so good!

Flash didn't really like coffee.

Flash enjoyed being a policeman.

He showed off his new badge
and blue hat.

Playing golf was lots of fun!

Putting was the tricky part!

Flash loved horsing around!

It sure beat hoofing it!

What a thrill!

Parachuting was very exciting!

Flash was really happy!

He loved roasting marshmallows!

Three big scoops!

Ice cream was fun to serve!

Happy Birthday Flash!

So many candles thought Flash!

Flash's Choice was a good nap!

He loved his hammock!
The End

Flash had so many choices. Only he knew what job he would choose and what games might've been his favorites.

Charlie is a jazz pianist and author. He lives in Ocala Florida with his wife Becky and of course his pal Flash.

To order additional copies of this book, contact:
Xlibris
844-714-8691
www.Xlibris.com
Orders@Xlibris.com

ISBN: 978-1-6698-6887-3 (sc)
ISBN: 978-1-6698-6888-0 (hc)
ISBN: 978-1-6698-6886-6 (e)

Library of Congress Control Number: 2023903625

Print information available on the last page

Rev. date: 04/13/2023

Printed in the United States
by Baker & Taylor Publisher Services